My Mom and Dad Don't Live Together Anymore

A DRAWING BOOK

For Children of Separated or Divorced Parents

by Judith Rubin, Ph.D.

MAGINATION PRESS • WASHINGTON, DC

To all the children who have taught me so much
about what it's like for them — JAR

Published by
M A G I N A T I O N   P R E S S
An Educational Publishing Foundation Book
American Psychological Association
750 First Street, NE
Washington, DC 20002

For more information about our books, including a complete catalog, please write to us,
call 1-800-374-2721, or visit our website at www.maginationpress.com.

Editor: Darcie Conner Johnston
Art Director: Susan K. White
Printed by Phoenix Color, Rockaway, New Jersey.

Summary:
A journal and drawing book to help children express, explore, and work through their thoughts and feelings
related to parental separation or divorce. Includes a Note to Kids and a Note to Parents about the value of
art therapy in coping with the emotional stresses of a family break-up.

ISBN 1-55798-835-8

Contents

A Note to Kids

This book is for kids whose parents have decided to separate or divorce. If that is happening in your family, you have already been through a lot. Whether you are reading this book yourself or someone is reading it to you, you probably understand most of what is in it, because it's based on what real kids in this situation have told me they think about.

There are many good books for children of all ages that can tell you about divorce and separation. This book, though, is just about you and your family. It is a place for you to tell your own story and to illustrate it, too. You are both the author and the artist of this book.

Each page is about one thing, like how you found out your parents were separating or how you feel when your parents are together now. Fill in the lines by writing in words yourself, or by telling the person who reads to you what you want him or her to write. Then draw pictures on each page to illustrate what you have said. Or draw first, then write—whichever you prefer. You don't have to do the pages in order. If you like, you can just read through and decide where you want to start. How you use this book, like what you say and draw, is completely up to you.

Since everybody's story is different, this book gives you lots of choices about what to say and draw. And if you want to change or add words so that the book is more about you, please do so. The important thing is to make this book your own, which means true for you.

This book can be private, or you can share it with anyone you feel comfortable with—a friend, a relative, a teacher, a parent. That's your decision. You can ask your parents questions about things you might not know, such as how they met or what you were like as a baby, but you don't have to. If you'd rather not ask and don't know for sure, you can just write and draw what you think happened.

What's most important is that you be as honest as you can, so that you can tell the truth about your own personal experience. Sometimes it's hard to be honest with yourself, especially about difficult things. But it's a good idea to try your best. The more you can tell the truth to yourself, the easier it will be to get used to all of the changes in your life, which is always hard for kids when their parents separate or divorce.

I hope that writing and drawing in this book will help you deal with all the changes. Even though you're not in charge of what's happening in your family, you are the "boss" of the words and pictures you put in this book. Creating them might also give you ideas for more pictures or stories. Then you could use any size paper and any art material—like chalk, paint, or clay— to express what you're feeling and thinking.

If you're having a really tough time, don't be afraid to tell someone. It might even help to see a therapist or a counselor—a person outside the family who can help you with all of the confusing feelings you're having. Of course, that's up to you and your family to decide. Maybe you're already seeing someone. If so, it will help that person to help you if you share this book with him or her.

Whatever you do, you should know that it's really hard for everybody to get used to the changes, no matter what age they are. I've been a therapist for 40 years, and I've seen lots of kids whose parents were separated or divorced. And I have never met anyone who said it was easy, including grown-ups!

So make this book your own record for yourself of what has happened in your family. Draw with anything you like, including markers, colored pencils, crayons, pens, and pencils. You can use different materials on different pages. You can add your own ideas to those in the book. And even though the thoughts and feelings that you are writing and drawing are serious, I hope that you will also enjoy creating your own book and that you will feel better about all the changes that you and your family are going through.

Me

My name is _____.

I am _____ years old. Here's a picture of me when I _____

_____.

In this picture _____

_____.

My Mom

My mom is_____ years old. Here is a picture of her when she _____

_____.

In this picture_____

_____.

My Dad

My dad is _____ years old. Here is a picture of him when he _____

_____.

In this picture_____

_____.

They Met Each Other

At first my mom and dad didn't even know each other!

They met when _____.

Here is a picture of how they met. In this picture _____

_____

They Liked Each Other

After my parents met each other, they liked each other a lot, so they

spent time together doing things like _____.

Here is a picture of my mom and dad going out together. In this picture

_____

_____.

They Got Married

Then my mom and dad decided to get married, so they had a _____

_____wedding, and it was_____

_____.

Here is a picture of the wedding. In this picture_____

_____.

They Were a Couple

At first, my mom and dad were a couple, just the two of them.

Here is a picture of them before they had children. In this picture

_____

_____.

They Became Parents

The first child my parents had was _____.

Then they weren't just a couple any more. They were parents too.

Here is a picture of when they first became parents. In this picture

_____

_____

I Was Born

I was the *first second third fourth* _____ *th* child in my
(CIRCLE ONE OR FILL IN THE BLANK)

family. I don't remember much about being a baby, but they tell

me I was _____. Here is a picture of me as a baby.

In this picture _____

_____.

My Whole Family

I am the *only oldest youngest middle* child. In my family there are
(CIRCLE ONE)

_____ children. The way I feel about my place in the family is

_____.

Here is a picture of my whole family doing something. In this picture

_____

_____.

A Happy Memory

There are lots of things I remember from before my parents

decided to separate, and some of them are happy. Here is a

picture about a happy memory of _____.

In this picture_____

_____.

A Sad Memory

Some things I remember are sad, like when _____

_____.

Here is a picture about a sad memory of _____

_____.

In this picture _____

_____.

A Scary Memory

Some things I remember are scary, like when _____

_____.

Here is a picture about a scary memory of _____

_____.

In this picture_____

_____.

How I Found Out My Parents Were Separating

I did not know that my parents were going to separate until_____

_____.

This picture shows how I found out, where I was, and who told me.

In this picture_____

_____.

How I Felt When I Found Out

When I found out my parents were separating, I had lots and lots of

feelings, like_____ and _____.

Here is a picture of me when I was feeling really_____.

In this picture_____

_____.

What I Felt Like Saying

When I found out my parents were separating, there were lots of things

I felt like saying. Here is a picture of me saying _____

to my_____ and how I imagine my_____

would react. In this picture _____

_____.

What I Felt Like Doing

When I found out my parents were separating, I felt like doing some

things, such as _____.

This is a picture of something I felt like doing, and how I imagine my

_____would react. In this picture_____

_____

_____.

What I Didn't Feel Like Doing Anymore

When I found out my parents were separating, there were some things I

didn't feel like doing as much as I used to, such as _____

_____. Here is a picture of something I didn't feel like

doing for a while. In this picture _____

_____.

How I Felt Toward My Mom

When I first found out my parents were separating, I felt _____

_____ toward my mom, especially when _____

_____. Here is a picture about that. In this picture

_____

_____.

How I Felt Toward My Dad

When I first found out my parents were separating, I felt _____

_____toward my dad, especially when _____

_____.

Here is a picture about that. In this picture _____

_____.

Why My Parents Separated

My parents *did*   *did not* tell me why they decided that they couldn't
(CIRCLE ONE)

stay married. I think the main reason was _____

_____. Here is a picture that shows why

I think they separated. In this picture_____

_____.

Sometimes I Worry It's My Fault

Sometimes I think it's my fault. Even though they tell me it's not, I still

worry that they wouldn't have separated if I _____

_____. Here is a picture of that. In this picture_____

_____

_____.

If I Could Fix Things

Sometimes I imagine what I could do to fix things so that my

parents would get back together again, like if I_____

_____.

Here is a picture of what I wish I could do so we could all live

together like we used to. In this picture_____

_____.

Sometimes I Blame Other People

Sometimes I blame other people, like_____.

At times I think that if_____

my parents might still be together. Here is a picture about that.

In this picture_____

_____.

The Move

There have been lots of changes since my parents separated.

The biggest change was when_____moved out of our

home, which happened_____.

Here is a picture of the move. In this picture_____

_____

_____.

How I Felt About the Move

When the move happened, I felt _____.

Here is a picture of me during the move. In this picture_____

_____

_____.

The Next Big Change

After that, the next big change that happened was _____

_____. Here is a picture of that change. In this picture

_____

_____.

How My Mom Has Changed

Sometimes I feel like my mom has changed. She used to be_____

_____and now she is_____.

Here is a picture of her. In this picture_____

_____

_____.

How My Dad Has Changed

Sometimes I feel like my dad has changed. He used to be_____

_____and now he is_____.

Here is a picture of him. In this picture_____

_____

_____.

A Change I Like

There have been lots of changes, and some of them have actually been

good, such as_____.

Here is a picture of a change I like. In this picture_____

_____

_____.

A Change I Don't Like

There have been some changes that I don't like at all, such as _____

_____. Here is a picture of a bad change.

In this picture_____

_____.

When My Parents
See Each Other Now

Since they don't live together anymore, my parents don't see each

other every day like they used to. In fact, when they see each other

now, it's often because of me, and I feel _____ about that.

When they do see each other, they act _____.

Here is a picture of how my parents act now when they see each other.

In this picture _____

_____.

How I Feel When My Parents Are Together

When I see how my mom and dad act with each other now, I often

feel_____. Here is a picture of what

I'd like to do or say at those times. In this picture_____

_____

_____.

How My Parents Used to Treat Each Other

I think my mom and dad treat each other *better   worse* than
(CIRCLE ONE)
before, when they were living together. Here is a picture of how

my parents used to act with each other. In this picture_____

_____

_____.

Having Two Homes

One of the hardest changes is that my mom and dad live in two

different places. Right now I spend most of my time with my_____

_____, because_____.

Sometimes I wish I could change things, such as_____

_____. Here is a picture about that wish. In this picture

_____

_____.

When I'm at My Mom's

When I'm at my mom's I usually_____.

Here is a picture showing me_____.

In this picture_____

_____.

When I'm at My Dad's

When I'm at my dad's I usually_____.

Here is a picture showing me_____.

In this picture_____

_____.

The Hardest Part of Changing Places

Going from one place to the other isn't so easy. The hardest part

is_____.

Here is a picture about that. In this picture_____

_____

_____.

The Best Part of Changing Places

The best part of going from one place to the other is_____

_____. Here is a picture about that.

In this picture_____

_____.

Keeping Track of My Things

Keeping track of my things can be pretty hard. Sometimes I need or want something that is at my other parent's place, like_____ _____. Here is a picture of what happened when I left my _____at my_____'s.

In this picture_____ _____.

The First Time I Told Someone

The first time I told someone about my parents not living together any

more was _____. I felt _____

about doing it. Here is a picture of me telling_____.

In this picture_____

_____.

How My Teacher Found Out

_____told my teacher about my parents separating.

I felt _____ about my teacher knowing about all

the changes in my family. Here is a picture about my teacher finding

out. In this picture_____

_____

_____.

Telling My Friends

I *have* *have not* told my friends about it, and I think that telling
(CIRCLE ONE)

them is a *hard* *easy* thing to do. I also feel _____
(CIRCLE ONE)

about telling my friends. Here's a picture of me telling one of my

friends, whose name is_____.

I think my friend was thinking_____.

In this picture_____

_____.

When People Ask Me Why

When people ask me why my parents separated, I feel_____

_____about answering that question.

I think it's *harder   easier* to talk to grown-ups than to other kids.
(CIRCLE ONE)

Here is a picture of me saying_____

to_____. I think they were thinking_____

_____.

In this picture_____

_____.

An Easy Person to Talk To

One person I can talk to pretty easily about the separation or

divorce is_____ , especially when_____

_____. Here is a picture of us together and we are

_____. In this picture

_____

_____.

Who Helps Me a Lot

When I think about people who have helped me with my parents'

separation, the first person I think of is_____.

Here is a picture of how_____helped me, by

_____.

In this picture_____

_____.

How Other People In My Family Feel

I'm not the only person in my family who has feelings about my parents'

separation. My_____feels really_____

about it, and I know because_____.

Here is a picture showing my_____'s feelings.

In this picture_____

_____.

When My Mom Talks to Me

Sometimes my mom talks to me about what has happened in our

family, and I often feel _____when she does

that. Here is a picture of when she told me_____

and I felt _____. In this picture

_____

_____.

When My Dad Talks to Me

Sometimes my dad talks to me about what has happened in our family,

and I often feel_____when he does that.

Here is a picture of when he told me_____

and I felt_____. In this picture

_____

_____.

What I'd Like to Say to My Mom

If I *asked told* my mom things I'm afraid to talk about, I would say
(CIRCLE ONE)

_____.

Here is a picture of how I imagine she would react, by_____

_____. In this picture

_____

_____.

What I'd Like to Say to My Dad

If I *asked told* my dad things I'm afraid to talk about, I would say
(CIRCLE ONE)

_____.

Here is a picture of how I imagine he would react, by_____

_____. In this picture

_____

_____.

My Grandparents on My Mom's Side

I call my mom's mother_____and her father_____.

(NAME)   (NAME)

They live_____, and I see them_____.

In this picture_____

_____.

What I Do With My Mom's Parents

When we are together we usually_____.

Here is a picture of us, and we are_____.

In this picture_____

_____.

My Grandparents on My Dad's Side

I call my dad's mother _____ and his father _____.

(NAME)   (NAME)

They live _____, and I see them _____.

In this picture _____

_____.

What I Do With My Dad's Parents

When we are together we usually_____.

Here is a picture of us, and we are_____.

In this picture_____

_____.

If My Family Was Different

Sometimes I wish that my family was different, like_____

_____.

Here is a picture of the way I wish things were in my family. In this

picture_____

_____.

My Favorite Daydream

Sometimes I dream when I am wide awake, and imagine things that might happen. Some daydreams are good ones that are about my wishes. My favorite daydream is _____.
Here is a picture of that happy daydream. In this picture_____
_____
_____.

My Worst Daydream

Some daydreams are bad ones, because they are about my fears and

worries. My worst daydream is_____.

Here is a picture of that scary daydream. In this picture_____

_____

_____.

What I Do When I Have A Scary Daydream

When I have a scary daydream, I usually_____.

If I want to feel better, I usually_____.

Here is a picture of something I do to feel better when I have a scary

daydream. In this picture_____

_____.

My Favorite Dream

Sometimes I remember dreams I had when I was fast asleep.

One of my favorite dreams was_____.

Here is a picture of that good dream. In this picture_____

_____

_____.

My Worst Nightmare

Sometimes I have bad dreams too, like my worst nightmare, in which

_____. Here is a picture of that bad dream.

In this picture_____

_____.

What I Do When
I Have a Nightmare

When I have a nightmare that wakes me up in the middle of the night,

I usually_____.

If I wake up in the morning after a really bad dream, I usually_____

_____. Here is a picture of something I do

to feel better when I've had a bad dream. In this picture_____

_____

_____.

The Future

So far, this book has been about what's already happened in my family.

I'm not sure what will happen in the future. I wish I knew! When I think

about what's going to happen I sometimes imagine _____

_____.

Here is a picture about that. In this picture_____

_____

_____.

If I Ask My Parents About the Future

If I ask my parents about what's going to happen in the future, my mom

_____and my dad_____.

Here is a picture of me asking my_____about

_____and what they would do or say.

In this picture_____

_____.

My Worst Fear

My worst fear about the future is _____

_____ .

Here is a picture of what I'm afraid might happen in the future.

In this picture _____

_____ .

My Biggest Hope

My biggest hope about the future is_____
_____.

Here is a picture of what I hope will happen. In this picture_____
_____
_____.

What I Can Control Myself

I know that even though my mom and dad can divorce each other, they

will never divorce me. I also know that even if I tell them what I want,

I don't have control over what they do. So I have to concentrate on

things that I can control myself, such as _____

_____or_____.

This picture shows something that I can do myself to make things

better. In this picture_____

_____.

What I'd Like to Ask Other Kids

If I talked to other kids whose parents are divorced or separated,

I would ask them _____

_____. Here is a picture of me asking

some other kids and what I imagine they would answer.

They are saying_____.

In this picture _____

_____.

If Another Kid Asked Me What to Do

If other kids asked me what they should do if their parents

decided to separate or get divorced, I would tell them to_____

_____.

Here is a picture of me telling _____

to _____and how I think they would react.

In this picture_____

_____.

What I'd Like to Tell Other People

If I could tell other kids or parents about what it's like when your mom

and dad decide not to be married anymore, I would tell them_____

_____. Here is a picture of me telling

_____ and how I think they'd react. In this picture

_____

_____.

My Advice About Separation and Divorce

If anyone asked for my advice about separation and divorce, this is

what I would tell them: _____

_____

_____

_____

_____

_____

_____

_____

_____

_____

_____

_____

_____

A Note to Parents

Separation and divorce are hard on everyone in the family. Children feel sad, worried, angry, and confused. They often feel somehow responsible for the break-up and may feel guilty about that. Often you, as one of the adults involved, are in so much distress yourself and have so much to do that you can't pay as much attention as you'd like to your children.

Since it is vital for them to stay as secure as possible in your love, it can be hard for them to be fully open right now — for fear that you might disapprove. Even if you are open to anything they might ask or tell you, they may not want to reveal all that they are experiencing. A journal, such as this drawing book, offers children a comfortable outlet for expressing and sorting through their thoughts and feelings. In addition, children usually have feelings and fantasies that they don't even know about, at least not consciously.

Drawing is a natural way for children to express themselves, especially when it is hard to find words that fit what is going on inside. I am a clinician with expertise in art therapy who has worked with children and families for 40 years — before, during, and after separation and divorce. As an art therapist, I know that some things are just easier to "say" with images than with words. Drawing and writing can give children a sense of control over, as well as relief from, difficult feelings.

Many excellent books about separation and divorce are available for parents and children of all ages. I strongly encourage you to buy such books for both your children and yourself. At a minimum, it can be very reassuring to discover that everyone experiences the same upsetting things that you and your children are going through. It is also helpful to learn about different methods of coping, as well as the feelings and behaviors you might expect in your children, and the healthiest ways for separated or divorced parents to interact on behalf of their children.

But even the best book about separation or divorce does not allow children to express their own feelings or to tell their own story. That is the purpose of *My Mom and Dad Don't Live Together Anymore*. It can provide a channel for releasing children's feelings, thereby relieving internal pressures. This should help to alleviate some of the inevitable pain, loss, worry, and anger that accompany parental separation and divorce.

If your children are old enough to read, please let them keep this book as private as they wish. The more honest they can be with themselves, the more useful the writing and drawing will be for them. If children are young and need to have the book read to them, it is vital that you respect their right to say and draw whatever they honestly feel, even though that might be hard for you.

Indeed, you may find your children's honest feelings upsetting. If you do feel uncomfortable or upset about what they write or draw, it is best to simply look and listen. Most important, don't try to talk them out of what they're expressing. What they need most from you at this time is acceptance, which doesn't mean agreement.

By all means, if what your children write or draw distresses you, talk it over with another adult, such as a friend, relative, clergy, or therapist. You deserve support for what you're going through, too. But it isn't fair to expect assistance from your kids, although it may be tempting, and they may even be helpful.

Although this book is addressed to children rather than parents, you might find it helpful to think about how you would deal with some of the topics yourself: what words you would fill in and what pictures you would draw.

People of all ages find relief and release by creating when they are under stress. You might be surprised at how helpful it can be. You can simply fool around with any medium you like, and create whatever comes to mind. Don't worry about being an artist. Just relax, give it a try, and enjoy yourself.

Using Expressive Media

For this book, markers (thin or thick) and crayons are good, although if your children prefer colored pencils, pens, or standard pencils, that's fine, too. It's most important that they use the materials they're most comfortable with, so let them choose.

It will also be therapeutic if you can provide other art media for free expression during this time. Whether you offer clay, paint, chalk, or anything else, simply choose things you can be comfortable with. Also, be clear about the rules for when and where art materials can be used, as well as the rules for clean-up.

About the Author

JUDITH ARON RUBIN, PH.D., is a pioneer in the field of art therapy, first working with hospitalized schizophrenic children in 1963. A past president of the American Art Therapy Association, she has worked as an art therapist and educator in many professional, community, and academic settings. She holds a doctoral degree in counseling, and has studied adult and child analysis. Currently Dr. Rubin is on the faculty of the Department of Psychiatry at the University of Pittsburgh, and the Pittsburgh Psychoanalytic Institute.

Dr. Rubin is the author of *Child Art Therapy* (1978, revised 1984), *The Art of Art Therapy* (1984), *Approaches to Art Therapy* (1987, revised 2001), and *Art Therapy: An Introduction* (1998). She is also the producer of three films about art and children, and was the "Art Lady" on *Mister Rogers' Neighborhood* during its first three years in the late 1960s.

Dr. Rubin has maintained a private practice since 1974, seeing patients of all ages in art therapy and psychoanalysis, including many children and families. She has three children and four grandchildren, who all love to draw. Currently, she divides her time between Florida's Sanibel Island and Pittsburgh, while working on videotapes about art therapy.

Dr. Rubin welcomes comments and suggestions from children and parents about this book. Please address correspondence to Dr. Judith Rubin, 128 N. Craig Street, Pittsburgh, PA 15213, or to Magination Press.

Related Books from Magination Press

I Don't Want to Talk About It, by Jeanie Franz Ransom MA, illustrated by Kathryn Kunz Finney, afterword by Philip Stahl PhD. Explores a child's feelings and reactions to the news that her parents are separating, and reinforces the message that parents love and care for their children as much as ever. Today's Librarian "Best Children's Resource" award. 32 pages, fully illustrated, available in paperback and hardcover. Ages 4-8.

What Can I Do? A Book for Children of Divorce, by Danielle Lowry MS, illustrated by Bonnie Matthews. Goes beyond "it's not your fault" and offers children real solutions and resources for dealing with the hard questions and feelings they face when parents divorce. 48 pages, fully illustrated, available in paperback and hardcover. Ages 8-12.

My Parents Are Divorced Too: A Book for Kids by Kids, by Melanie, Annie, and Steven Ford (as told to Jann Blackstone-Ford). Wisdom, advice, and comfort about divorce, parental dating, remarriage, and blended families from kids who have been through it. American Booksellers Association "Pick of the Lists" award. 64 pages, with photographs, paperback. Ages 8-13.

The Case of the Scary Divorce, by Carl E. Pickhardt PhD, illustrated by Jeff Fisher. Explores a boy's feelings of anger, jealousy, fear, and loyalty in the wake of his parents' divorce. 96 pages, with illustrations, paperback. Ages 8-13.

MAGINATION PRESS
750 First Street NE
Washington, DC 20002-4242
To order by phone, call 1-800-374-2721.

80